Europa
editions

Elena Ferrante

The Beach at Night

Illustrations by
Mara Cerri

*Translated from the Italian
by Ann Goldstein*

Europa Editions
214 West 29th Street
New York, N.Y. 10001
www.europaeditions.com
info@europaeditions.com

Copyright © 2007 by Edizioni E/O
First Publication 2016 by Europa Editions

Translation by Ann Goldstein
Original title: *La spiaggia di notte*
Translation copyright © 2016 by Europa Editions

Library of Congress Cataloguing in Publication Data is available
ISBN 978-1-60945-370-1

Ferrante, Elena
The Beach at Night

Book design by Emanuele Ragnisco
www.mekkanografici.com

Printed in the USA

Mati is a five-year-old girl who talks a lot, especially to me. I'm her doll.

Her father has just arrived—he comes to the beach every weekend.

He's brought her a present—a black-and-white cat. So until five minutes ago Mati was playing with me and now she's playing with the cat, whom she's named Minù.

I'm lying on the sand, in the sun, and I don't know what to do.

Mati's brother is digging a hole. He doesn't like me. He cares more about a booger than he does about me, and all the sand he's shoveling he dumps on me.

It's very hot.

I think about the last game Mati played with me.

She had me jump, she had me run, she got me scared, she had me talk and shout, she had me laugh and even cry.

When we play, I chatter a lot, and whatever I talk to answers me. But here, by myself, half buried under the sand, I'm bored.

A Beetle passes by, so busy digging himself a pathway he doesn't even say hi.

Mati's mother left the beach an hour ago and went home. Now her father, too, is about to go; he's loaded down with bags.

"Mati, let's go, hurry up."

Mati heads off from the big beach umbrella along with her brother and the kitten.

And me?

I can't see them anymore.

I call out: "Mati!"

But Mati doesn't hear me.

She's talking to Minù the cat; she hears only him, and he answers her.

The sun has set, the light is pink.

A Beach Attendant arrives. His eyes, I don't like his eyes. He folds up the big beach umbrellas, the chaises. I see the two halves of his mustache moving over his lip like lizards' tails.

Then I recognize him.

He's the Mean Beach Attendant of Sunset—Mati's always scared when she talks about him. He comes to the beach when it gets dark and steals the little girls' toys.

The Mean Beach Attendant is very tall.

He calls his friend, the Big Rake, who's even taller than he is, and together they start combing the sand.

The Mean Beach Attendant of Sunset sings a song that goes:

Open your maw
I've shit for your craw
Drink up the pee
Drink it for me
Sh-h-h! Not a word
Only traps are heard
Peace will come
If we all play dumb.

The Big Rake has horrible iron teeth, shiny from use. He bites the sand ferociously as he advances.

I'm afraid—he'll hurt me, he'll break me.

Here he comes, he's here.

I end up between his teeth along with pumice-stone pebbles, shells, plum and peach pits.

I feel a little beat up, but I'm all in one piece.

The Mean Beach Attendant goes on singing in a threatening tone:

Off with your nose
On the pot repose
Clear out your throat
You won't stay afloat

Everything he raked ends up in a pile of sticks, sand, tissues, bags, and plastic bottles.

I've been flung down not too far from a plastic Pony, a metal Bottle Cap, a ballpoint Pen, the Beetle that passed a while ago, digging, and now is on his back, waving his legs.

The light isn't pink anymore but violet. The sand is cooling.

I'm very sad, and angry, too.

I don't like this cat Minù, in fact I hate him. Even his name is ugly. I hope he has diarrhea, and vomits, and stinks so much that Mati is grossed out and gets rid of him. By this time I should have had a bath with her, and be at dinner with the whole family, eating from her spoon, a mouthful for Mati and one for me.

Instead I'm here, belly up like this Beetle, and I have to listen to the horrible song of the Mean Beach Attendant of Sunset.

It's getting dark. There are no stars and no moon, either. The sound of the sea is louder now.

It's damp, I'll catch cold. Mati always tells me: "If you catch cold, you'll get a fever." She says it exactly the way her mother says it to her. Because Mati and I are also mother and daughter.

So it's impossible that she's forgotten me. As soon as she realizes I'm still here on the beach, she'll certainly come and get me. Maybe it's just a game she invented to scare me.

The Mean Beach Attendant is very annoyed. He kneels down beside me and says to the Big Rake:

"We didn't even find a gold bracelet, or a necklace with precious stones. There's just this ugly doll."

"I'm not ugly!" I yell.

The Mean Beach Attendant stares at me with his cruel eyes. He strokes the lizard tails of his mustache. Then he extends his gnarled, dirty hands, picks me up, tries to open my mouth, shakes me.

"She still has words in her," he says to the Big Rake. Then he asks me: "How many did your mamma put inside you, eh?"

I hide at the back of my throat all the words Mati taught me, the ones we use for our games, and I stay very quiet.

"Let's see. At the doll market they pay a lot for words that come from games."

The Big Rake appears to agree and sticks his teeth out even farther, as if to open up my chest. But the Mean Beach Attendant of Sunset shakes his head no.

He clicks his tongue and from between his lips a small Hook emerges, like a raindrop.

The Hook, hanging on a disgusting thread of saliva, drops down until it enters my mouth.

I quickly collect all Mati's words and hide them in my chest. Only the Name she gave me stays behind.

The Name is very frightened, it calls itself: "Celina!"

The Hook hears it and, wham, grabs it and rips it out of me—it really hurts.

I see Celina—my Name, the Name that my Mati gave me—fly through the air attached to the Mean Beach Attendant's saliva and then disappear beneath the lizard tails, into his big mouth.

But he's disappointed—the Name isn't enough for him. He shakes me hard.

"Just Celina?" he asks. "That's all?"
The Mean Beach Attendant hurls me angrily into the brush. I end up near the plastic Pony, the ballpoint Pen, the Beetle. I hear him ask the Big Rake:

"How much will they give us for a doll's name? two bucks? three?"

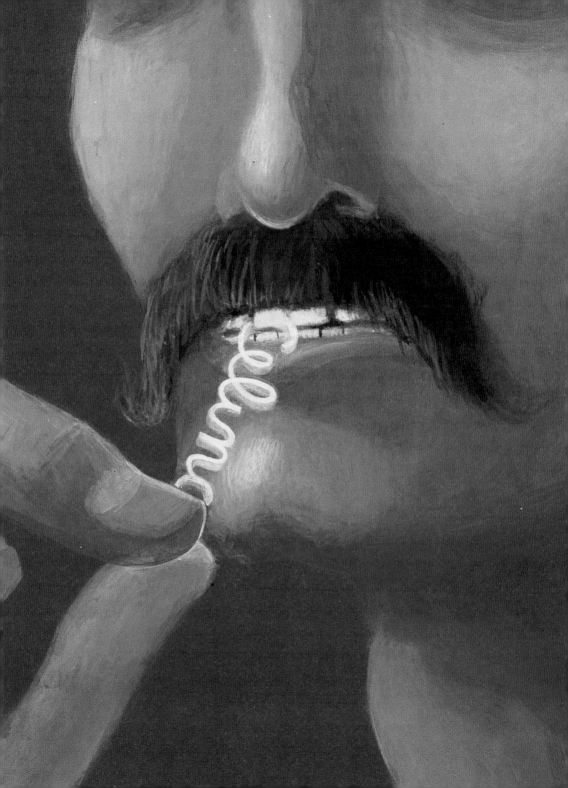

Ah, how sad I feel.

The Name that Mati gave me is lost forever. Now I'm a little doll without a Name.

But I keep quiet, I don't say a word. The Mean Beach Attendant is still here, a tall dark shadow.

His voice has started singing again:

Next to the wall
See darkness fall
Like an illness
arriving wordless
The voice is missing
The fire is hissing
Celina, farewell,
Ugly as hell.

He kneels down and lights a match. It makes a nice warm little flame. He touches it to the dry wood, which immediately catches fire. Then he gets up, looks for a minute at the burning twigs, and goes away, holding the Big Rake in his right hand.

Now I feel better.

It's warm, I don't feel the dampness anymore, and I won't catch cold.

But I see that the Beetle is worried, he's turned himself over.

"What's happening?" I ask.

He hurries away from the light of the Fire and I don't see him again.

The Fire is pleasant company. Every so often he sputters, *psst*, then crackles contentedly and throws out red sparks.

I also hear the sound of the Sea, which has grown even louder.

A Wave comes and goes, like an elegant lady, with a white fringe of foam.

"Are you going to get me all wet?" I ask.

"*Bro-am!*"

"I don't understand."

"*Bro-am!*"

"O.K., say whatever you want, what do I care if you get me wet?"

The Fire is burning pleasantly, getting warmer and warmer.

I shout to the plastic Pony: "It's nice here, isn't it, Pony?"

I call to the ballpoint Pen and the Bottle Cap:

"Lovely evening, wouldn't you say?"

But I realize that the metal Bottle Cap has turned flame-red and the ballpoint Pen is writhing, as if he's pooping black ink, and hissing:

"*Frrrrisss.*"

That upsets me.

In alarm I say to the Pony:

"Pony, we have to do something. The ballpoint Pen is sick."

But I discover that the Pony, too, is suffering. His mane and tail have melted in the heat. His mouth has become a hole as big as his head. Suddenly he shouts "*Bok*" and disappears in a reddish-blue flare. How terrible! The Fire is burning everything, he'll burn me, too.

"Fire," I beg, "please, don't burn me. I'm Mati's doll, she'll be angry."

The Fire immediately turns toward me and clicks his bright red tongue:

"*Ooam!*"

So I turn to the Wave:

"Help, Wave. I'm Mati's doll. Remember how when our bottoms were all sandy this morning we washed them off in your water?"

The Wave beats hard against the black shore.

"Bro-am!"

As if that weren't enough, I hear the Mean Beach Attendant of Sunset returning, and he says greedily to the Big Rake:

"Did you catch that? The doll is talking like crazy. Hurry up. Tomorrow we'll sell all her words at the doll market and we'll be rich."

Now I am really and truly scared.

As long as Mati was there, I would talk to any object, any animal, and it would answer in a clear and reasonable way. If people or things or ugly creatures behaved rudely, we yelled at them and they stopped. Even when boys wanted to hit us, kiss us, see our underpants, pee on our feet with their little dickies, we knew we'd win in the end.

But now?

Without Mati, I don't know how I'll survive.

The Wave is talking, but I can't understand him.

The Fire is sticking out his tongue, and wants to burn me just the way he burned the Pen and the Pony.

The Mean Beach Attendant and the Big Rake have already taken away my Name and now they want to steal all Mati's words. What if I turned into a stupid mute doll, or one who only says the same recorded words all the time?

Mati, Mommy, where are you?

I'm your doll, don't abandon me.

You know what, Mati, if you don't come and save me right away, if you let me burn, I'll cry.

The Fire finally did it. He leaned forward and grabbed me by the hem of my blue dress.

He went "*Flusss*," and now the material is burning. It has a nasty smell.

"Bad Fire," I chastise him, but he repeats "*Flusss*" and spreads even farther, till he brushes my hand with his boiling breath.

The Mean Beach Attendant tries to grab me with the Big Rake, who sinks his iron teeth into the embers to pull me away, spraying sparks as he goes.

I think for the last time of Mati, in her cool bed.

I think how nice it is at night to be cuddled against my sleeping mamma. It won't ever happen again.

I'm sure she's sleeping with her cat now. Her love for me is over.

I don't want to be captured by the Big Rake.

I'd rather burn, keeping in my chest the words of my games with Mati.

Naturally.

Instead the Wave arrives.

He's a lot bigger. His white mouth, at the top of a restless body of dark water, flies over me and crashes down on the Fire, on the Big Rake, shouting:

"*Brooo-aaam!*"

When the water hits the Big Rake's red-hot teeth, he exhales a white cloud of steam.

The Fire goes out, too bad for him.

I'm about to say: "Thank you, Wave."

But I'm already starting to roll over, dragged by the Wave.

Everything rolls: shells, pumice stones, the metal Bottle Top, coals, charcoal, the Wave, me.

I end up in the Sea.

"Mr. Sea," I say, "you were very kind, you and your Wave, to save me, but now take me right back to the shore, thank you."

The Sea doesn't answer. But even if he answered he wouldn't be able to grant my request.

The Night Storm has risen on the Sea.

The Storm is a lady in a long dark-blue dress. She wears a crown of Lightning on her head and has a booming voice, because Thunderclaps are continually coming out of her wide mouth.

The Sea, churned up by the Storm, is like the water in the bathtub when, at home, Mati and I make a rough sea and the waves slosh over onto the floor and Mati's mamma comes in and cries: "Out of there right this instant: look at the mess you've made."

But here no one comes.

I'm all alone.

I don't even recognize the Wave anymore.

There are so many waves now, running after one another and fighting to see which is the tallest.

So I pray:

"Please, Mrs. Night Storm, please calm down. Mr. Lightning, don't blind me. Mr. Thunder, don't deafen me."

And on the beach the Mean Attendant, in a furious rage, shouts at the Big Rake:

"Did you hear her? She's still talking, we've got to get her!"

Meanwhile the water in my mouth goes down into my stomach, and I sink.

Down, down, down I go.

I touch the bottom.

I end up amid Fish, Tin Cans, broken Bottles, two Crabs, a Starfish.

I lie down on the sand. It's comfortable.

The Night Storm has become a distant rumble. The water is moving gently, like Mati when she rocks me.

How much time has passed?

I'm as mute as a fish, a crab, a starfish.

The words that Mati taught me are quiet. They float inside my chest, inside my stomach. Sometimes they swim up to my mouth, but silently, like words in books or in Mati's mother's head when she's reading and doesn't want to be disturbed.

How peaceful.

But here comes a Hook.

The Hook is as tiny as a raindrop and it's attached to a shiny thread of saliva.

It drops into my mouth, which is always open. I'm so full of water I can't pull my words away in time to hide them in my chest and my stomach.

The Hook grabs one and tugs. The other words, terrorized, cling to one another, forming a chain.

I pull from one end, the Hook pulls from the other, and in the middle are the words holding tight to one another.

I'm furious. I've lost my Name, but I don't want to lose anything else.

With these words Mati and I were happy.

With these words she talked and had me talk, had the animals talk, had the stars talk, the clouds, the grains of sand, the sea water, the lightning and thunder, the beach umbrellas and the chaises, everything.

If the Hook attached to the disgusting thread of saliva takes them away from me, I won't remember anything, I won't know how to say anything, not even the dear name of Mati.

The Mean Beach Attendant of Sunset and the Big Rake will sell them in the market and I bet that cat Minù will buy them all.

The Hook gives a sharp jerk.

The words, holding one another by the hand, move rapidly toward the surface of the Sea.

I've barely got time to clamp my mouth around the last remaining word: mamma.

With my teeth clenched tight around mamma I go up, up, up. While I rise toward the surface, hanging from my own words, I hear the spiteful voice of the Mean Beach Attendant of Sunset singing at the top of his lungs:

The tongue I slice
Right off, in a trice
The names I seize
With the greatest of ease
Together we sing
Treasure for a king
For affection I pine
On delight I dine
Your heart I'll shred
Until it's dead.

The disgusting thread of saliva stretches thinner and thinner, until there's a last tug that spits me out of the water along with the screaming chain of Words.

The night is ending.

I fly through the orange air of Dawn, my teeth clenched around the "MA" of mamma. And I'm about to drop onto the sand when a Dark Animal runs by. He grabs me in his teeth and keeps on running.

The Hook shoots off, the thread of saliva breaks. The words return to my mouth with a snap, like an elastic band.

The Mean Beach Attendant of Sunset loses his balance and falls on the sharp iron teeth of the Big Rake.

The Mean Beach Attendant of Sunset cries "*Ow-ow-ow*," and he is still crying.

But the teeth of the Dark Animal are gentle.

The Dark Animal hardly bites at all, he warms me with his breath.

We run over the beach, which is all wet because of the Rough Sea and the Night Storm.

Luckily the sun is rising and everything will dry off.

The Dark Animal has long whiskers that tickle me.

We are running through the pinewoods.

I hear the birds singing, the faint thump of the pine-cones falling on the dry needles. I also hear the desperate crying of a little girl.

I know that cry.

The Dark Animal's breath gets warmer and warmer. He leaves the path, climbs up the trunk of a big cluster pine, flies along a branch, and jumps right through an open window.

Here's the little girl who's crying.

She cried all night, her face is red and bathed in tears. Neither her mother nor her father nor her brother could console her.

The little girl is Mati, my Mati.

She calms down only when the Dark Animal lays me carefully on her bed.

"Celina!" she cries, and hugs and kisses me.

Oh joy!

Mati's parents go back to sleep.

Even her brother, who is always so grouchy, lies down on his bed and falls asleep. Now he's snoring.

"I'm so glad you came back," Mati says to me.

"Me, too," I say, and right away I tell her: "Do you know I was almost killed by the Big Rake and the Mean Beach Attendant of Sunset?"

"I know," says Mati, who always knows everything, like a perfect mamma.

Then she turns to the Dark Animal with whiskers and, full of emotion, says:

"Thank you."

"You're welcome," he says. He smiles at me, and holds out a paw.

"A pleasure: Minù the cat."

"I'm Celina," I say.

"What a pretty name!" says the cat.

"Minù isn't bad, either," I say.

I'm so happy to have found my name again I can even be happy about his.

To Matilde… to Bagni Elsa in the eighties
M.C.

ABOUT THE AUTHOR

Elena Ferrante is the author of *The Days of Abandonment* (Europa, 2005), *Troubling Love* (Europa, 2006), *The Lost Daughter* (Europa, 2008) and the four installments of *My Brilliant Friend*, known in English as the Neapolitan Quartet (Europa, 2012-2015).